A collection of short stories

Gopal Patra

pencil

ISBN 978-93-5610-434-1

Published in India 2022 by Pencil

A brand of
One Point Six Technologies Pvt. Ltd.
123, Building J2, Shram Seva Premises,
Wadala Truck Terminal, Wadala (E)
Mumbai 400037, Maharashtra, INDIA
E connect@thepencilapp.com
W www.thepencilapp.com

Author biography

Gopal Patra: -

The life of a poet-storyteller is an invincible soldier who fought in battle - whose tool is fearlessness and honesty ... Search Google for details and type in Bengali or English letters. If you search "Gopal Patra" you will get all the information.

Address :-Gopal Patra
Vill- Bhagabati Pur
P.O - Chaturvuj kati
P.S - Shankrail
Dist- Howrah
Pin Cod - 711313
West Bengal - India

Mobile number9143098660

Email address:-patragopal561@gmail.com

Facebook link:-
https://www.facebook.com/profile.php?

CONTENTS

A collection of short stories

A collection of short stories
Gopal Patra

Dedication:- All neglected people.

A collection of short stories

Inthe last few years, four short stories based on true events have found a place in this collection ...

Here are some social stories that have received reviews from various online magazines and groups in my own timeline.

Those stories, respectively

1) **Greatempathy**
2) **Prostitute**
3) **Witch**
4) **Heredity**

From these stories you will get a glimpse of the present life… just as the socio-economic aspects are highlighted in it, so the neglect and hatred towards people is equally evident!

Now if my readers like it, I will consider my work successful!

Gopal Patra

Author's biography

Gopal Patra:-

The life of an impeccable poet-storyteller, an invincible soldier who fought in the war - whose tool is fearlessness and honesty ... Search Google for details "Gopal Patra" Or "Gopal Patra" in English Search "Gopal Patra" and you will get all the information.

Address :- Gopal Patra
Vill- Bhagabati Pur
P.O - Chaturvuj kati
P.S - Shankrail
Dist- Howrah
Pin Cod - 711313
West Bengal - India

Mobile number- 9143098660

Email address:-patragopal561@gmail.com

Facebook link:-
https://www.facebook.com/profile.php?

Table of contents

" Great sympathy"

(The story of oppressed, exploited and deprived people)

Farmers, sharecroppers, day laborers, coolers, blacksmiths, fishermen, weavers, cobblers, scavengers, day laborers, who are the main driving force of our society, without whom our conventional life is almost unimaginable. But how is their life? How do you spend their days and nights? That is the story of their lives.

The exchange of broken bones day and night brings us all the necessities of life and in return What do the people of the upper echelons of the so-called society see in their eyes?

People are not considered human beings They cheat in many ways.

Those who cultivate the gold crop do not have rice in their stomachs at one time - they do not wear clothes in one go! Or even a drop of medicine for treatment. There is no place to hide in winter or rainy season. What kind of society?

Chapter One

Harihar and Kashinath, two brothers, live at the far end of Fatehpur village with their wife, son, daughter and old mother! Due to the lack of eco-land, at the end of the village, there is a small space on the side of the road and there is an edge with bamboo poles.

All the burdens of the world are now on Harihar .. Wife - has a three year old son and a one year old daughter! Kashinath is not married yet! The father has been in the hall for four years now - so it is up to them to see the widowed mother.

The house is very low - there are two rooms in it .... Due to the heavy rains of the last two years, the thatched roof of the house has rotted and turned black - this year how Harihar can't think about the rainy season but there is no way to change the hay.

The straw that Boro planted last year has been burnt due to lack of fuel. Aman paddy was not cultivated this year due to lack of money.

Now it will take one hundred and fifty rupees to buy straw from somewhere and press it in the house .. where will you get it?

Harihar did not make a mistake in trying to get a loan from anyone but who will lend them straw? What if they can't repay the loan? Still no one to touch ... Finally ...

Harihar appeared in the courtyard of Tin Kari Ghoshal .. Mr. Jatha about him ... After much pleading, Harihar read the real word ... I was saying, will Jathamshai lend me two or three straw? The roof of the house is rotten, it is raining in front, so don't say ...

I will give good luck as soon as the rice rises next year! I have not cultivated this year, so if you say please give me two or three hay, then it would be better ....

I can give you two or three rupees in a whole haystack ... but when I borrow it, take it ... Bapu ...

And if you lend it or if you just burn it, you will end up burning straw ... then will you buy me? Where can I get money?
I have not wasted any time.

Will you sell the land again?

I saved three bighis of land for food ... I will eat the remaining one bighi again?
Now that the rice is rotten, what should I do?

I'm not sure if I'm going to be able to do that ... but I'm not going to be able to do that ...
Tell me, where did Go go, big wife? I say he is shouting Kenu village ..

Why are you so angry?

And I'm just calling, is it?
So this is what I heard ..
I am coming now ... I have gone somewhere else ..

At that moment there was another knock on the front door ..
Ms. Ghoshal was annoyed and said in her mind that Chulo who came again that morning to annoy?

This is a bastard with no bones left in the air ...
Thinking this, he slammed the door open and announced three ...

He opened the door and saw a widow standing with her clothes torn and dirty. Her face was dry and pale. There was ink in the corner of her eye. Let him do what he has so much lenadena? Annoyed, he asked, "What do you want?"

You came to show your dry face at seven o'clock ... What can I do?
As much as ...

The widow, after being harassed by all these unpleasant questions, pointed to the gold bracelet in her hand and said.

You give me some money by keeping the bala dukhani ...

If my only daughter is not very sick, maybe she will survive! After saying this, the widow's eyes filled with tears. Ghosalamshai began to weigh the weight with his hands.

Still, Kachumachu said, what will be the price? I see gold leaf on copper ...

But let's see how much can be given ...
He entered the house saying ...

After a while Ghosalamshai came from inside the house with a similar bracelet and said - there is very little gold in it, I can pay about five hundred rupees! Nehat your daughter is very sick so .

I will give you five hundred rupees again ... maybe if you don't give me you take your thing - don't bother me .... I have a lot of work to do ... Hari hey Give friends ...

The widow thought in her heart that she could earn at least a thousand rupees by selling Bala Dugachha. It will come in handy in times of danger but when he says putting gold leaf on copper ...

Maybe - he would have taken Bala Dukhana back but the money he needed so much ... the boy would have died if he had not seen the doctor - and there is no treatment without money - Bala is not more expensive than a boy - After thinking about such five seven, he agreed to sell two bracelets for five hundred rupees.

After a while Ghosalamshai gave money to the widow He showed a white paper and told the widow not to tip here - the widow did so What's your name?

Amla Bala- said the widow ... After receiving the money, the widow left for home ... On the way home, the widow remembered that 65-70 years ago today, during her marriage, her father gave her a dowry as a dowry.

But today he has to sell because of scarcity. One year from today, his son is suffering from tuberculosis.

And all the brass-casa that was in the house to see the doctor is gone ... so he sold the only memory bracelet pair of father's house without looking for any other way ... he had no regrets - if the boy survives ...

He had been carrying a pair of bracelets in a small basket for so long that no one else knew ...

He came to the front of the house remembering all these things - the sound of the boy's whooping cough came to his ears - and he entered the house and saw the pillow getting wet with blood on his face.

Next to him, his daughter-in-law is sitting like a madman with her hands on her head. But mom didn't respond ...

maybe there was no food in the house- so maybe she couldn't think what to say to her son!

The eldest son probably went to the doctor Babu. He came home and cried. His grandmother Amla Devi asked, "Did the doctor come?"

No ... the doctor said I wouldn't go if I didn't pay the rest ...

Will your father get better when I go?

Am I God to make your father better? Do you have money to buy medicine - to feed that father? And your father will survive? I couldn't take the medicine which ...

You have 60 rupees left before you bring the income, but I will go! Naren cried and said these words- how old will he be 9-10 ... he has not studied so much in his forehead.

Heard about this Mars in the face of the doctor came home and cried! He knew what would happen to the world if he was a 9-10 year old boy. Because if you don't give the rest of the money, you won't come to see his father because he is a great doctor.

As soon as Amla Devi heard this, a fire started burning in her eyes.

Naren took the money from Grandma and rushed to the doctor ... About twelve o'clock he reached the doctor! Doctor Babu saw Naren and said why are you here again?

I said I can't go ... This time I came with money or I came empty handed ... If I don't get money, I will not go ...

Naren gasped and said, "Take your money ... My father's excess is too much for you to go once ..."

ChapterTwo

Doctor is coming to treat Naren's father who is about to do his duty after receiving money in advance.

What happened to the paper that signed that tip? Why did you take the tip signature from the widow? What does Ghosalamshai do? Does he work or not, etc ...

Quickly signing the paper, Ghosalamshai took it to Manmath Babu - he kept the account of Ghosalamshai sin and virtue ..in terminology he is called Naibamshai! A good witness will also be found to do the work with Manmohan Babu .. Thinking this, he said - I will write whatever I say and leave it in the chest ... He started saying.

I sold my dugachha gold bracelet for 5000 / - (five thousand rupees) in cash from Ghoshal Mahasaya on 5th Ashar 1395 for my son's illness! Iti Mrs. Moni Mala Bala Devi
(Tip above signature)

Witness: - Monmath Roy Dated 05-03-1395
This is the business of cheating people ... Because his body of great mercy ...

But he was illiterate so he had to keep Manmohan Babu - to keep accounts - to write a will! The poor peasants of the village used to come to Mr. Ghosalam to mortgage pots, pitchers, brass and bronze things and get some money in return for the time of scarcity

...

but the tied things would not go back to their homes! Because for a long time the interest rate would have been higher than the price of the thing due to having things tied up so things could not be released.

And if someone came to borrow money empty handed, he would give it at high interest rate ... at compounded rate And he wrote down more than he could borrow ...

If you give an example, you will understand what kind of business. If someone borrowed 5 rupees, he would write down such a name. Borrowing 50 rupees from me by keeping such and such person as witness at such and such address Nilen etc etc ...

And when that man came to pay the money, Joe would not have disbelieved, then he would open the book and show how much money he had borrowed ... how much money has been in interest till date! Joe would not have disbelieved if the book was opened.

If he had disbelieved then he would have had to admit that there was no way to say anything on his face thinking that if he did not lend money later ...

If anyone disbelieved, he would announce three cowries ...

He would show how great he is by touching the garland of Hari - and he would curse by touching the garland - he would curse and say that you will not be well at all ...

You see - God will punish you - He will help people in distress Hearing all this today? God bless you ...

Take any accurate information or calculation of how many people have been put in the way by these various excuses ... They are also called vampires .. aquatic capitalism ... consumerism ...

Chapter Three

At this point, Naren's father's condition became worse and worse! It is three o'clock in the afternoon,

I have not seen Dr. Babu yet .. but will you come back after eating and drinking?

Yes, that's right .. the doctor arrived at 3:30 in the afternoon .. Standing in the yard hesitantly began to think whether to enter or not to enter?

If you don't mind entering the house then what you hear in the mouth of the neighbor will not be of any use ...

because Naren's father's heart is stuck in the boat - even if he doesn't want to, he has to go to the other side ...!

However, let's see once again - once he stopped the telescope in the patient's chest and gave an injection and said in a sad face - there is no hope - he can no longer be saved ...

The widow is standing in the corner of the room with her head bowed ... The lady is sitting with her hands on her head as if she has become a stone and can't hear anything!

And when she comes to him she is going to say whatever she can in harsh language ... Rakshasi - The witch is playing with her husband at such a young age ... Nothing is getting into her ears -

With only half-dead eyes, tears are falling and clothes are getting wet ... that little boy is crying to his mother for food ...

Uncle Naren ran to call his cousins ...

Some people are going to see Naren's father for the last time - coming! Naren's father's life bird flew in the sky as soon as the evening lamp went out in the afternoon ...

Only the bones made of blood and flesh were left ... The shadow of mourning descended on the whole house-

Mother Kakima Jethima Local women started crying loudly ... Some people started calling the new widow as witch-demon-demon! Because Naren's father died at the age of forty-one -

So all the blame fell on the new widow ...
No one will understand that he was a farm laborer. If there was no work, he would not have joined, he would have spent the day fasting - fish and meat have never joined his forehead.

It was not possible to earn a living by working for five days alone ...

Let him go now, he will not have to fast anymore - now he will sit on the golden couch and enjoy the great

pleasures
But what will his ten or eleven year old son Naren do?

His widowed mother - old grandmother - with his younger brother Ramesh - will he be able to feed them?

How can a father do honest work?

Will he borrow money at high interest from people like Tin Kari Ghoshal? And if you can't pay, will you sell the last resource and come to the way?

And is there an alternative?

Chapter Four

As usual, the rain queen came and spread her thick black hair all over the sky ...

Tapur Tupur plays an anklet all afternoon who is like a Kajla girl ...

Today is a rainy day .. You donated the first step of a rainy day ...

How many such songs are peeping in the heart of the lover-loyer .. Birhi Yaksha Parabat who is sending a letter - to his beloved ...
How many pigeons are spending their honeymoon in their house ...

Khichuri in Dhoni's house - Hilsa fish market is making the air smell ...

How many jasmine buds have blossomed in the twigs of Kadam ...

The body woke up in the wind ...
Meanwhile, the house is floating in the water due to the rotting straw of Harihar's house ...

Maybe one day he will have to stay up all night with his wife, son, brother and old mother!

There is no shortage of snakes, frogs and insects to house on the side of the road - they have to live with them because they are not human ...

Just a creature that looks like a human being - what do they have to do with human identity? They are street dwellers - poor day laborers .... to the society they are unclean untouchables and little people.

In Harihar's mind, maybe today they would not have to sit in their way if their father had not passed away prematurely ...

For the last three years, the father has passed away with all the burdens of the world on them - but how can he bury his father? Who will lend them?

Many people wanted to borrow money but to no avail - some people said they would bury their father by borrowing money.

Meanwhile, if the order of the foremen of the body does not work properly in the society, they will be kept in one room!

Excluded from the society will be expelled from the village .. Then the rule of the society is that on the day after shraddha all the people of the neighborhood should be invited and fed ...

Brahmins should be fed .. Otherwise it will be bad for the society! And the newly widowed fish-meat-egg will not be a place of hell if it is banned forever!

There were no well-wishers to rely on the intellect and even if there was, it doesn't seem to be profitable! Because if you want to do honest work, you have to obey the orders of the foremen - so one day with a call for drinking -

Dad's Shraddha to discuss how to have peace - how to be saved from this danger ... After some talk one of them said - Ki Hari Do you have to do everything according to the rules of society?

In that order ...

Harihar's words were snatched away and another one said, "Listen to me, sir. I have to say yes or no. If not, why do you live in the society?"

And why did we come? To get to our dock - do we have to pay?

Many people supported him and said yes, yes, we have to do it.

After many such conversations, a foreman said, "Have you raised any money?"

And there is only one week left - or empty handed ...

Harihar's little uncle said, "Will you sell the thing on the ground or not?"

Harihar said in frustration, "If not, I don't see any other way."

As if there is no defect in the work - then even if your father dies, you will not get peace.

One of them said, "You will not live in the house and do the work of a father. What happened to that?"

During these conversations, a foreman said to Hari Har, I will sell it. Have you seen any customer letter? Hearing this, Harihar said,

"Where is such a thing?" This is what I was waiting for ...

Then he said feeling a little hesitant but how much should I pay?

I could not touch the sky ... so now that everyone is there, if you fix the price .. then it can be taken! What do you all say?

Everyone supported him. Harihar thought it was better to give it to his uncle than to sell it to others.

The thing including the house was cut. All three of them agreed on the price - 1500 rupees.

Everyone said in unison that they are paying a good price - what will be the price of three katha place? Moreover, who will pay so much money in this untimely danger?

Kakababu said, "Okay, I will pay the money three days before Shraddha."

What else can be done? In front of everyone, a raw will was made by taking out a sheet of paper ...

Kakababu happily took the will paper in his hand and said - of course you don't have to leave the house immediately - you can stay for two-three months ... Do you have to make a place like a head?

We all have to agree on what we have decided together ... We have to agree - if we don't agree, we have to stay in one house - we will not allow anyone to work on the land and if we don't work on the next land, how will they work?

They are farm laborers ...

Chapter Five

Aman paddy rice is in full swing ... Harihar has only one bigha of land… it will be completed soon ...

If you don't have to work on other land, not a penny will come home ...

Because they are farm laborers - they have to work on other lands to earn gold! So they have cultivated their land according to some way ... they have gone out to work in the field in two ways ... otherwise how will the family survive?

What makes the stomach move?

Fasting can not be saved for long! Of course, it is not that they do not have the habit of fasting. However, Harihar's old mother and son's food is collected anyway.

The work of the field laborer is not always available again ... for about three months you have to sit quietly with your hands folded and again the work is interrupted due to natural calamities.

So in the working season, they spend the night with their two brothers, sometimes they stay in a double bed, because if they don't save some money, will they eat at home?

Fifteen or twenty days have passed since the cultivation of

aman paddy was almost over - then small jobs will be found ... Then how can

I feel that they have spent three or four months, no one knew except themselves and the one who has come to this world.

This time it was Aman's turn to cut the paddy How does this money go?

One more month has passed without eating ... The time has come for Harihar to cultivate Boro paddy.

Then it will be the food of the year - no matter what, you will be able to eat twice as much rice ....
After a while I thought our resources are one bigha of land - will any of us share the land?

He thought to himself that he should try with courage, thinking that he should share the land with many people, but no one agreed to give him the land.

Again some people said- if I give you land, what will I do to cultivate the land- fertilizer - what do I do .. those who are tired of bringing salt will cultivate the land again? Who will give the land?

I haven't been able to give you rice in the end ....
When it did not help to reach out to everyone, I remembered Kanai Mitri, a rich man with a circle next to him.

Harihar used to work on his land most of the time .. Mitri held Moshay's hands and feet and prayed that two bighas of land should be given to him for share cultivation ...

Mr. Mitri said in simple language - that six bighas of paddy per bigha ... must be paid immediately after harvesting! Don't listen to any objection ...

He said again that I said six moons per bigha ... if you can tell me? If not here's a new product just for you ...

If Harihar thinks that land will not be available anywhere else .. he agreed thinking this! At that time, if the land was cultivated, the zamindar had to pay four to five manas of paddy per digha.

But since Harihar Mitri pays the wages on Moshai's day - his throat is full - his family survives on the wages ...

so some sympathetic family needs to be informed, thinking that According to the rules of society, you have to pay a little more ... because you have to pay whatever you say without protest ....

What does it matter if they eat it or not?

People from the upper strata of society?

Living in the palace, sitting on the floor of the fan day and night, watching the color TV spends the day in great joy!

They no longer have to work in the fields, sweating in the sun and water - what do they need to know about the poor street laborers on the ground floor?

Are they of any use to the upper class? They work day and night. To sustain their lives .. At their own urging - burning their stomachs ....

then you judge the peasants - the laborers the laborers - the farm laborers what is the benefit to the people living in that palace? Small people carry big people for their own sake ... don't they ....

So why would a group of big people try to understand the news of their happiness and sorrow?

They themselves are happy, but can not sleep at night! In society, they can live with their heads held high!

No one protests their words! Seeing them, everyone bows their heads! Anyway, at least he didn't go down without explaining himself first.

Of course I cursed him in my heart ... I can't come to him! When what they want to get may appear unintentionally, will they benefit from the news of the working people? What do you say?

Chapter Six

If the land was found, it would have to be cultivated this time ... Harihar had saved two hundred and fifty rupees during his work without feeling like eating ..

Two brothers with one or two laborers worked day and night and lost three bighas of land.

But this is not the end of it. Regular watering is required. Weeds need to be cleaned.

Fertilizer should be given at the right time. Pesticides should be applied in case of disease and insect infestation. Moreover, there are natural calamities.

Meanwhile, the price of tractors to cultivate the land is left! So one day, one or two nights, Harihar and his brother Kashinath wake up in the fields with olives and go to work in other lands ...

because they have to live by eating - they have to fertilize the land at the right time.

There is some money but the mother has to see a sick doctor because if he travels to Amritlo at this inopportune time then maybe their only resource is to sell the land to one side ... his mother seems to be suffering from a serious illness for a long time ....

A great doctor should be shown - but those who do not have a double food alliance again a great doctor? When it was a little over, Girish used to bring medicine from the doctor to Apara and somehow to get rid of it. Yes!

But the land was not fertilized on time .. After a while, the weeds were not cleared - if the manure was given by cutting the land in a double cut and making some kind of namo namo.

There is no way to clear the weeds - Because now that room doesn't have a single particle - it's all gone! If you do not work on the other land, the water will not be collected! In the meantime,

I had to fast for two or three days because I could not go to work because of the heavy rain.

Chapter Seven

The next day Harihar went out to look for a job ... but could not find a job.

Mitri Moshai finally reached Mitri Moshai and told him that Mitri Moshai has some work to do in his garden but if he does not do it now ...

. Who told Mitri Moshai that they are fasting for two days ..

Hearing this, Harihar said that if Babu had given some advance, mother and son Ramu would not have had to go hungry! So what if I had some money in advance ...

There were tears in Harihar's eyes when he said these words. Mitri noticed this, so he lowered his voice a little and said- I am giving you five rupees in advance ...

but remember, I will not go to work on someone else's land, but come tomorrow ...

After buying some flour and some sugar, Harihar somehow started walking towards the house. I entered the house and saw some data being boiled ... What can be done?

Kashinath had cut all the data from some kachu trees on the side of the road after seeing the delay in returning to

Hrihar's house.

Hariya assured that he would return after collecting some food ....

so seeing Harihar not returning, this arrangement! Harihar spent a few hours on the flour he had brought - the widowed mother let the little boy eat it mixed with sugar because they could not just eat the flour hour!

They spent the day boiling the little data themselves.

The first week of the month of Chaitra during the time of paddy harvesting ....

Now there is no work in the field. Or work for low wages! If not, what will happen? Bidhatai knows how long it takes to spend half a day eating half a stomach of boiled kachu data ....

The paddy has started to bear fruit in two or four days. At this time, it is necessary to irrigate with good water. Irrigation is not given in time because water cannot be drained from the chimney.

And Kashinath, who is not to blame, his body is not a stone - what if it looks like a black stone?

What will happen if his body is made of blood and flesh and is soaked in this sun-burnt water and the soil is cut from morning to evening?

Plus the food never got right ...

The paddy that has borne fruit - of course no one has had such a good harvest ... First of all, lack of water - good tidal water has not entered the canal this time to fill the soil ...

Diseases due to bad weather - Insect infestation was high.

Another special reason is that when the paddy started to bear fruit, there was a heavy hailstorm - many flowers fell in it ...

as a result many stalks were destroyed - moreover, many stalks of paddy fell to the head of the rice plant - the head was broken!

And I don't need to explain that Harihar's paddy is the worst.

Anyway, the paddy is ripe now. It has to be taken to the house ...

Harihar and his brother have somehow cut it up and taken it to the house - now he has to be released - meanwhile the zamindar has sent the man to take the news. In case he sells it to someone or if he eats it too late, he sends Ramesh to find out ...

In the morning, Ramesh Harihar who said- Kiri Mitri Moshay sent rice when dibi?

Do you understand that I have just picked up the paddy and what will I eat if I don't work in the next few days?

So come after a decade ....
When the paddy was sifted, it was seen that the mind had grown twenty-two paddy in three bighas of land ...

Will you give it to the zamindar- and who will have their own?

What to eat all year round? Such are the thoughts of Vivo's Harihar when Zamindar Mitri Moshai came at that time ....

I think he got the news from someone that the paddy has been threshed so he showed up without any delay - there was no doubt that he had come to get the paddy ...

So his chest trembled because he watered the raw blood of his chest and with great difficulty he produced this little crop ...

Now the zamindar will take everything away ... So his voice became like a voice - he wanted to burst into tears but to whom will he express his sorrow and who will understand his sorrow?

Harihar said in a very moaning voice looking at the paddy shots I got this piece of rice ...

If I gave you bar mon rice - would we have it? What shall we eat? On hearing this, Mr. Mitri said, "Why are you working so hard ..."

One day there was no rice, but did you fast? Why should I keep fasting?

Mr. Mitri said .. So Khabi will survive by eating - I have said before giving the land,

I will not listen to anything! I don't care if it is paddy or not - if I don't have to give my paddy, do one thing, I don't want paddy, leave your land with me, I will cultivate till the price of paddy goes up.

Oitukui land resources will not work in any way ...

So what is the way to measure the amount of paddy?

People came with Mitri Moshai and brought the van with the rice sacks in the van. Where did Kashinath come from?

He hugged his legs and said many more things but he could not understand it due to the emotion of crying. Why did you go to me?

Nehat works on my land so I kindly decided to cultivate so much drama that I would give ...?
Kashinath started crying loudly while lying on the ground ...

Chapter eight

After a while, Harihar hugged his brother and said, "Brother, the day laborer, poor and helpless, has given us grief in the same way, Bidhata Afuran has also given us hunger ...

but has not given us the right to express it ... so we have to live our life in this way. The day too ....

This is how we were born and this is how we will die - slavery in the next land ... this is our deed, this is our religion and this is our lineage ....

My story is over ...
and the nine trees are twisted ...
But dear readers, I leave the following question to you ....

People for people, Life is for life. Can't people get a little sympathy?

And friend 8. People for people, Life is for life. Can't people get a little sympathy? And friend 8. People are for people.

People make people products, People make a living. People make people products,

People make a living. When the old history comes back, will you not be ashamed? And friend ..

People for people, Life is for life. Can't people get a little sympathy?

He is a friend. People are for people.

Tell me your loss The deepest river of life, If you are a weak person.

Tell me your loss The deepest river of life, If you are a weak person.
Man if he is not man Monsters are never human.

Man if he is not man Monsters are never human. If monsters are ever human, won't you be ashamed?

And friend
People for people, Life is for life. Can't people get a little sympathy? He is a friend. People are for people.

Special Note: - Lyrics and melody of the song and artist Bhupen Hazarika
****

" **Prostitute**"
is the story of a helpless woman ...

Oneof the stories of a woman who came to work from the state of State of Bihar to become a prostitute!

Do women really grow up to be prostitutes or prostitutes? Probably never.

Our society is largely responsible for this!
Many are enrolled in this profession because of the environment and the situation -

or they are only employed in this profession for the sake of their stomachs, that is, for putting food in the mouths of boys and girls.

And the biggest asset of femininity is selling at the price of water - chastity - Value-honor is everything.

The main character in this story is Jhumri. Trapped in a love affair - in the promise of work and marriage - finds refuge in the state of Bihar Purulia forest department post bungalow.

There, a few days later, all her femininity and chastity were looted overnight.

Then after drinking water from different ghats - Tourists visiting the city from that post bungalow –

To make fun of the gods She works to provide supplies - sometimes honeymooning with them for a little extra money.

But as a result of lockdowns across the country, post bungalows have been closed and livelihoods have been cut off.

How is Jhumri now?

What is the current condition of all those helpless and lonely women? Do this story with that story prostitute.

I hope everyone will like to read the story - one of the society You will find the dark side - and in the dark you will find the direction of true light.

Chapter One

After lunch and a little rest - I just left the post bungalow ...

The purpose is to enjoy the natural beauty - and this is the hope if some writing materials are matched in By chance.

White clouds in the blue sky of autumn - the game of sunrise is going on everywhere - trees and as if smiling - the green ceremony is all over their body.

I have chosen this solitude because I will absorb the natural form and juice alone! Deportation from friends can also be called voluntary deportation.

In the last two days, we got up at the post bungalow of Purulia Forest Department with some friends.

Truth be told- In a long lockdown - from sitting at home, the hands and feet are getting rusty, the mind and soul are panting -

Hearing this, my friend Sumon spontaneously said- Let's not go out anywhere.

I said - Where to go? Now the Corona era is not over.

He said - let's not go to a secluded forest - where there are less people - meaning less coronary panic.

On the same day, Sumon obtained a phone number from Sturist Magazine and booked two or three rooms in Purulia - a post bungalow.

This is just a few days, only two weeks to get permission to open the post bungalow.

But the tourists are not coming that way so the forest department authorities have arranged some discounts for some of the tourists if they come before the Pujo holiday season.

In fact, without any effort - without binding, the key to a few hotel rooms came to us almost at the price of water!

There was a worry in my mind that the hotel would match at a very low price - who knows what that would mean?

But I came and saw that it is not bad - the rooms are very comfortable and the other arrangements are also very good - that is, the bathroom, the kitchen, the room is clean and tidy.

And the food and drink arrangements are also good - the local adivasis cook for the tourists like Fife Ramash - the cooking is hand-cooked and very tasty and nutritious.

Some of us mean Sumon is also his girlfriend Priya- his girlfriend Shubhamita Ajay and Nandita and I am poor alone. We've all come out together - but they're in pairs - to blend into the deepest solitude - maybe to be one in mind or Anything else can be easily reunited -

because in this secluded forest there is no fear of man or wild beast except the call of two or four birds… two hot bodies or hearts open. So there is no obstacle in the match - let's be united in all the matches - what is the harm? No one cheated on each other!

I don't like that So the lone traveler.

Chapter Two

After a while, a hilarious smile came to my ears looked back and saw a lady following me - and from her face fell a mountain of words.

I have been walking indiscriminately along the rows of shawls - mahua - palash without giving so much importance -

After walking like this for a while - who knows what magic that lady came very close to me - mixing Hindi and tribal language - My purpose is stated.

Why are you alone baby?

Which partner do you have?

Lema is Hama's partner - Saying this, he spread that chaotic smile again - the solitude of the forest land was broken - it was eaten - it was echoed in the mountains.

The whole jungle is trembling with his smile as if is my chest trembling so much?

The loneliness of this deep forest is the only chaotic woman...

and it is normal for me to feel the trembling in the chest of a young man of twenty-five or twenty-six, isn't it?

If you do not call Shravan's ban on the chest and the blood in the chest gurgled as if for a moment.

Wearing old lehenga work-lehenga-eyes - all over the lips - low cost fancy cosmetics ... age around 30 - not beautiful but not bad body shape.

It took me a while to see him upstairs - so he said again. Didn't Babu Hummer answer that big- are you Babu Boba or not?

Laugh again ... I'm kidding Ray Babusab some lais karis la.

I said anxiously - Why not think of something?

And I'm not alone with my friends.
Yeah Al that sounds pretty crap to me, Looks like BT aint for me either.

And Hami also knows - all your friends who have taken their partner out In pairs - I mean, there are seven daughters of the dead.

How do you know
I know, babu, that is my job.

I said in amazement - what do you mean?
That is the meaning of Lai Babu - the service of the Babus of your Motan city - the supply of your supplies is the work of Hummer.

He understood - then it was good - what services do you provide?

Dorka all kinds of services to make you have fun - I mean native ducks - Banu - chicken - hariya - distilled wine and girl man - will need to give sob ...

Surprised, I said girl man?

Yeah Al that sounds pretty crap to me, Looks like BT aint for me either.
What does a girl do?

When I heard this, he laughed again - as if he had heard something strange from me.
He stopped laughing and said ...

You're a real spit fire and that's exactly what we like on this site CC! You are a boy So you asked this question?

Is it a job of a human being - work? All kinds of cam-dhanda yamon rannabanna kore dibe tuhade mauj - mastir somay peg banai! Out of curiosity I asked again - What else?

What else?

If you hand over a few rupees, Sohag will spend the night with you.

Where do you get all these supplies from?
What can I tell you, Babu Saab?

In this Jangalmahal, you will be hungry for the rest of your life.

He understood that you are their broker?
Babusab laughs as much as I hear your words are getting a lot of laughter… what bully hami broker?

Yes, Hami is a broker? But who took the burnt stomach and who took Hamara Balbachcha Palle.

A search baat bol babu sab a samaj me kon dalal neyi ho?

In this world, everyone is a broker-leader-minister-police-hamara.

I thought to myself that it is true - why don't you look in that direction brokers and brokers.

The whole world is full of brokers!
Did Babusab go silent - why are you talking?

I turned around and said, "Well, your name is still unknown."

What's your name

Hummer's name is Jhumri Babu.
Well, Jhumri used to say, why are you following me? I mean, why are you following me?

What are you doing? My old man has two children.

What is there to follow?

You are a big fool, Babu Saab ... even after telling you so much, you don't understand where is Hummer's mind?

Hami, I was looking at you from afar, and when I saw that your companions were walking in pairs one by one,

I saw that you were alone, so I followed you. Does Babusab like this lonely sister alone? So I followed you.

Janis babusab hamar bura marad do - bal bachcha sukha mara jabe ...

I wondered which of his eyes was blinking - I said why die dry?

Lockdown Babusab: The post bungalow was closed due to Maran virus Hamara kam dhanda sab chaupat ho gaya.

In this forest Yo Jori-Butia V Sob Khatam -
A leak of curry and a little bit of Danapani is also Lai Babusab.

I wondered why the government does not give you grants or rations.

Babusab will be a liar if he doesn't say yes - but the head of that ration dealer Geram and the head of the panchayat are united and steal most of it - he gives some of it to Babusab who doesn't pay the whole amount!

The reason he followed me for so long was clear to me. But Jhumri does not need my partner? All right, Babu Saab, what else can I do?

I'll leave. Speaking back Started moving.
My mind was filled with darkness remembering the dirty face of Jhumri in the middle of the moment…

Chapter Three

Will her husband and children really die without eating?

Or is it just a performance?

I will not be trapped in any trap or chakravyuh?
What exactly is a poor woman doing to me? What can trap or throw?

Let's not show it by doing a little experiment- let's not show it with courage ... Come on a trip to this jungle If a written logistics match.

That's why I called - don't go to Jhumri - listen.
Jhumri almost ran away when he heard my call.

Babusab said you will give me your Patna korbi?

I miss you anymore - have you been joking with me for so long?

All of a sudden he started saying these words again with a sigh.

Yeah Al that sounds pretty crap to me, Looks like Hummer aint for me either.

Why don't you go to Hummer's house, Babu Saab?

I said helplessly - all will be well, then the moment will come… now let's walk together a little bit, how to talk about happiness and sorrow?

After listening to me, Jhumri said, "It's all right, Babu Sub.

Hey no no ... how much do you have to pay?
Today, after a long time, I found you as a partner, so I will say more. And in my house I bought a hundred rupees.

I was shocked to hear the rate and began to think in amazement - how deadly the fire of hunger brings to this destructive form in this hilly forest floor.

A woman agrees to sell her best assets, the best ornaments, for only fifty-one hundred rupees to an unknown urban babu.

However, in this lockdown, sexual intercourse between men and women is a thing of the past - it is forbidden to show the faces of men and women.

But I understand that they have died and been defeated by the hunger of their stomachs.

Seeing me keep quiet for a while, Jhumri said - What is happening to Babusab Jada Mone? All right, whatever you want, so why not buy La Hoy Dis then go to the deep forest in Hummer's house?

How far is your abode?

Jhumri showed his hand and said that he was going to see the road on the left side and he walked to Hummer's house.
All right, then you stay.

Yeah Al that sounds pretty crap to me, Looks like BT aint for me either. This is not a good jungle.

Don't worry about the money, if you can make me happy, I will be happy too - then you can buy whatever you want.

Chapter Four

So far, the indigenous people of Jhumri - after hearing the messy language mixed with Bengali and Hindi - what kind of suspicion did I have?

Jhumri seemed to be stunned to hear the unanswered question on my face - then said with a sad face -

Loy Babu Saab My Bihar State May Ghor Thi - He was a neighbor of that post bungalow for a long time. He was a neighbor of Hamer.

After arriving there, Pahale worked for a few days at Dakbanglo - meaning Hama had to do everything from cooking to sweeping.

A few days later, one night, the head of the caretaker Grammar, along with a few other babus, knocked me unconscious. Hummer looted everything - threw a breath naked in the forest behind the post bungalow.

In the middle of the night, all the people of Gremer saw Hama in that condition.
The old man is now dragging the stove and lying dead on the ghat in Hummer's house.
On hearing this, I said that you did not protest or the police.

Jhumri said with a laugh - and protest Babusab - who will listen to whom? In this jungle palace, where is the last face of Mukhiya - the police are thuto jagannath here - Mukhiya was also with them that night - but innocent Budhiya was punished!

That's the decent thing to do, and it should end there.

Hummer man in the name of Bad V and Bura - I had to be the mistress of that chief for a few days.

Then the first child was born I will join the work to procure the material of Mauj Masti and if there is any opportunity, I will get some money.

And from then on I went to the forest from Lachhmi to Jhumri Whore Hummer is a brothel.

Babusab hamar kutha to sunali tuhara kutha kuchu bal ta babu tu sadhu sudha?
I didn't mumble, I didn't have much luck -
I mean, I didn't join the alliance.

That's pretty babu then your first meeting?
I don't know what to say.
O Babu, you are so ashamed that -

I understand that I will destroy you today....

Chapter Five

After walking a bit like this, I reached Jhumri's house. It was evening - it was pitch dark all around. My mind is also getting darker thinking about Jhumri's life - her lifestyle - seeing her residence.

But how many ladies live like queens in the same profession in the big bars or bars of the city - whether they are film star models or housewives - the same profession is beds or prostitutes.

Let's not show what happened in the end when I came so far?

A small leafy hut shaded by forest herbs Beside him was a small cot in a hut of a smaller size, and in it a man was constantly stroking his hair - perhaps the old man of Jhumri.

The doorbell looks like a low-watt bulb burning inside the room - the door slammed shut ড় a small wooden plank with a boy lying on it - and a seven- or eight-year-old girl on a small floor with chalk on a slate. Cutting.

At a single gesture, Jhumri, a fourteen-year-old boy and a seven-eight-year-old girl,
immediately left the house.
Jhumri swept the bed of Taktaposh for a while and then told me that Babusab came and this is Hummer's camp.

Enters the room in a daze.

Asen Babu came to all the beds -
I had to sit on the bed - I saw that Jhumri was wide open - meaning the top of the langar was undressed.

Come, Babu, come to Hummer's chest - this jhumri will give you some energy today.

I stared at it for a moment and saw Jhumri's fleshy breasts-breasts-thighs all over her body, the claws of a ferocious animal - as if some ferocious animal had bitten her! Of course the wound is dry now -

It is not difficult to understand the cause of this wound. Lockdown. The animals are afraid of him. So today Jhumri is wounded but not bloody.

But how to extinguish the stomach irritation of hundreds of women?

So after overcoming all the obstacles, we have to go to the ghat to catch the baby like us.

Honestly, I have come to this bed only to get writing supplies... but I have no desire to play with a woman's dignity for some money.

I was not only surprised to see the face of Jhumri's body, I became speechless, not hate - my mind was filled with tears of pity.

Seeing me being silently beaten, Jhumri said, "Babu, do you see me like that?"

Now everything is dry.

Janis Babusab has been suffering from this burning stomach for two or three days.
Bidhata Hama is still alive because the girl is the life of the people.

But Babusab, what do you think so much? If it was another man, he would have eaten me with such a twist and a twist.

Jhumri's words sounded unbearable to my ears - so I said without delay, put on your clothes now, Jhumri.

Seeing my body, you feel disgust, Ray Babu is getting sub bomi?

But why with Eli Hummer?

My son thinks that his mother has found a good customer and that he can eat well. Lai must die without eating.

So they left the house with a gesture of humming করে who knows what will happen to them now, ignoring the wildlife?

And now you are breaking our agreement, baby, you see, you will be fine.

I saw that his eyes started burning like two tigers in anger.

I went very close to Jhumri and pulled her head to my chest and told her to calm down. Listen to me.

But not the exchange of your body!
But Babu, I have nothing but this burnt body that ...

Then you do one thing, baby, sub-eyes, understand or show that - we are massaging your feet, hands, whole body, head - you will see that all fatigue will go away.

I said in an annoyed voice, "I don't need Jhumri Osbe."

But I will serve you right now, Babusab.
You were saying on the way that for the tourists.

All kinds of supplies mean domestic ducks and wild chickens

You don't have to procure all that - we will cook for a few days while we are there, buy a little more so that what is left and who will be able to bring that leftover food to your house and eat it with your husband and children… how?

Hearing my words, Jhumri's crooked eyes started flashing - tears of joy were shed, maybe that's all.

He hugged me and said how good you are, Babu Saab.

I said that the experience in your life can make everyone in the society feel bad!

But did you know that some good people are still there today because the moon and sun are rising and the earth is spinning - flowers are blooming in the forest Isn't it?

You are right Babusab you are right.

I want to live and love people like you, Ray Babusab ... Greetings to your birth mother. With one and a half thousand rupees, the rest will have to be withdrawn from the ATM tomorrow -

I told Jhumri that it was okay - now leave - I'm getting late - this is your five hundred rupees in advance ... and I gave five hundred more to raise the domestic ducks and wild chickens - come to Bengal tomorrow morning but ...

Jhumri carefully took the money from me and put it on her forehead - she greeted me again and again.

I said come on then.

Jhumri said go carefully Babusab.

I said don't worry I have a touch light I'll just get there.

I came out of Jhumri's camp - after a while I heard Jhumri's loud voice A few shops that buy ...

I saw Jhumri's sons and daughters walking silently from the opposite direction towards their destination, to their mother - to their mother.

The coughing sound of old man Budhiya is still spreading in the air in the sky of Purulia all over the jungle.

Finished...

" Witch"

Harishpur Village - Most of the people in the village are uneducated! Ordinary people in the village are working hard ... What will happen if their minds are white, they have become black with superstition and superstition!.

Not everyone in the village is a believer in superstition - there are some educated people who do not have the courage to stand up against superstition - they sit quietly in the house with their hands and feet folded for fear that the village elders will put them in a room! It's just a matter of hearing with your eyes and ears and feeling a little frustrated.

Name Kamala Devi Age It will be fifty-five - the color of the skin, the black eyes, a little bit of sitting - the distracted vision - the teeth can be said to be a bit big, uskokhusko hair... And to say that the dress is a half-dirty white cloth, in it again two-ten tappi dies and in mourning-grief, as if fifty-five feet have stepped.

For the past few years she has been divorced - the pain of losing her husband she almost forgot about her two sons!
But what absolutely happened is unbearable, even after hundreds of attempts to forget - the pain that no one but girls can feel - is the death of a little boy.

Amal died suddenly at the age of fifteen or sixteen days with a fever!

Mothers who are bereaved of their sons know what grief is like for their son. Even Bidhata herself cannot understand it - especially the pain of losing her son prematurely from a young age of fifteen to sixteen years so much that only he who has lost his son can understand.

Mother lost her way happily and sadly - her chest burst open and she wanted to become a bitch but it didn't break so much - only two eyes started shedding tears ... the time came when the tears stopped and the mind turned to stone.

When a person is sad. He expects so much sympathy or sympathy from others and when he sees that everyone is a partner in his grief... everyone is as sad as he is, then he finds solace and tries to forget the grief.

But instead of empathizing with the sympathy of this son Bihagini's mother, slander! This is not new to her. Many slandered her at the death of her husband but many times more than her at the death of her son. Some called her a vampire.

Instead of sympathy, instead of sympathy, listening to the bitter words, what happened is that the look is more horrible, the corners of the more open eyes are full of ink and the hair is rough and dry, it is dripping from the tip of the lips for winter, ha-ha. Many dare to talk to him and no one can turn away from him.

Seeing such a look and appearance, all the villagers got the idea that she was a witch - a demon - who ate her own son

- and if she looked at anyone else, she was no longer safe.

Most of the hardworking villagers had such an idea in their minds that if someone goes out for a good deed and confronts him, he will not go to the good deed anymore - if he goes to any house, the man of the house sees him and closes the door.

If a child sleeps on a cradle at home, the witch is removed from the cradle and hid in the house as soon as she sees him coming.

If the witch somehow appears while sitting down to eat, she leaves the plate of food and immediately gets up. If someone is sick, the fear does not come out.

All in all, from eight to eighty, there was a panic in everyone's mind, everyone was scared to see him... and when they went to a house trying to avoid him, they beat him up or kicked him out.

Although Kamaladevi's head was not right, she could understand everyone's behavior, so she would not go to anyone's house lest they be harmed - she was not afraid to see him - so she would not go out during the day or sit quietly in the house! At night he wandered about like a madman on the street or around a house, looking for someone.

Amal and Nitai were two friends a little away from Amal's house Amal and Nitai were two friends and they were about the same age and had some similarities! He used to look at her with wide eyes and whisper in his mind who knows what he could say.

Sometimes Nitai thought of Amal and wanted to hug him. Many people have seen this incident with their own eyes. That's when he called Nitai home and told her all about the witch.

Amal's mother killed witch and Amal - she sucked blood and ate it - you shouldn't go to her and call her as much as you want - she knows mantra tantra. ?

He wanders the streets in the sand - then if he falls in front of him, the great danger will suck all the blood.

Hearing these words on his mother's face, Amal's faith awoke in his mind. Amal's mother is really a witch - and Nitai's mind was filled with terror!

That's how Nitai's skinny patka looks - Vitu - Rashi is light then she is suffering from jaundice now she is very scared by her mother's words - normally weak people are more afraid than normal healthy people - all the fears she has should hug her!

The witch is worried about Nitai's jaundice, so she goes to her mother from time to time.
Hearing this in the boy's mouth, the witch spread her legs and started crying loudly. What will happen to me?

The witch's eyes are on my daughter.

It is as if a garland of roots of a tree is hanging around Nitai's neck or it will become jaundice - jaundice has increased to take Thakur home for treatment.

As the jaundice matures, her body becomes weaker and weaker, and the fear of the witch overwhelms her. At night, Nitai sometimes wakes up screaming that she is a witch, having nightmares. There was no doubt in the minds of the parents that the witch was watching over their son and was weakening him by sucking blood.

On that day Nitai Baba Kanai went to Kamaladevi's house on the advice of some Matabbars and threatened her eldest son Sasthi Charan saying that he would keep the witch in your house and he would harm the whole village.

It will be a bad day if you keep it tied - and if something happens to my son, I will not keep my mother and son whole - I will say this, I don't remember how much.

The news that Nitai had a witch's eye made him realize that there was no one left, and a commotion broke out all over the village. She had leprosy.

He is the uncle of the house next door to the 6th Charan. He thought it was probably a normal wound.

It seems that the wounds are not getting better as a result of the witch's vision, but they are getting worse day by day.

All the blame falls on the witch as soon as any disease of the neighborhood is cured or dies… people come to the

house day and night and curse - the people of the neighborhood are responsible for the blasphemy - in general, the witch has become a witch all over the village!
Listening to the complaints in the name of mother day and night, Sashticharan's ears got rotten, so what could he do?

If his mother is tied up, it will be good for the society, so be it.

Sixty feet when mother is shackled and crying, they call you a vampire, someone calls you a witch, or you keep an eye on their boys - and their illness - they are complaining to me every day, they keep you tied up, you believe, mother wants you tied up. -

I can't hold back the tears when I say this and I believe you can't be a witch or a witch - but I have no choice but to listen to them and believe them. Or tell me where I will go without grammar?

Will you let me stay wherever I go?

So you have to keep it tied up, mother, you don't mind - she would look at her face when she heard her son's words and she would be free to let go of her eyes - no one knew about her illness -

Amal, the son of his son who had lost a serious illness, was released from captivity one night and once went to their house to see Nitai.

Nitai was sleeping in the room with her mother and the bureaucrat was watching Nitai with wide eyes when Nitai's mother woke up and saw that the witch was standing behind her. Started.

Ogo, what is the defeat?

What will happen to Go?

Where is Go?

Neighbors came one by one to hear Nitai's mother's screams, thinking that something had happened.

They thought Nitai understood something had happened because his condition was not good.

Some of the neighbors came and thought that the witch had sucked the blood for that reason - and some of them thought that she might have died - Nitai's mother and the other neighbors cried then.

After a while Nitai regained consciousness but remained as he had fallen - no one could understand that his life was over! After seeing all the incidents, many people rushed towards Kamaladevi with broom shoes.

Then, as soon as the news spread in the village, it created an atmosphere of panic in everyone's mind.

There was no doubt in anyone's mind that the amla goddess witch had gone to eat Nitai's blood at night.

Two days later, one afternoon, Nitai flew into the sky, then he disappeared into space! Not only the whole village but the whole area was in an uproar and everyone was angry with the witch.

Many people think that he got angry after eating shoes and brooms on that day, so he killed them with mantras without any delay.

Besides, who killed Kanai's son Nitai today may kill someone again tomorrow - so it is not too late to kill that old witch today! And if her eldest son interferes, she too will be killed.

Everyone supported the word of the great foreman after receiving this order, one ran to Ojha because if Ojha is not near, the witch will suck the blood with the mantra tantra -

but if there is Ojha, the witch will not be able to do anything! Amla Devi was forcibly tied up and brought to a field at the far end of the village. Just in time, Ojha came. You can kill without fear.

At this order of Ojha, the angry crowd jumped on the orange deity with all the shoes and broom sticks they had in their hands…

then?

Then all that happened was that after a while, the weak body fell to the ground in a state of happiness and sorrow.

The villagers are happy to hear that the witch has been beaten to death like a dog today. On hearing this news, only one person's chest trembled but he could not cry. Everybody who died today on a happy day. Only one person had two tears in his grave....

" Heredity"

(Heartbreaking based on true facts .... A short story)

Sir is the blood exchanged here?
The receptionist of Nursing Home looks up in amazement ...

I can see when a woman of 30-32 years of unreal body has entered inside! With a boy of ten to eleven years.

What is thalassemia?

No ... Blood cancer .... No ... But?

No, I want to change all the blood on my son ...

I will collect all the money it takes! Without wasting so much time, he ordered the security to get the woman out, including the boy!

In this way, in the morning, in the afternoon, in the afternoon, in the afternoon, in the evening, at the door of the nursing home in different hospitals, the mother is knocking on the door with her ten-eleven year old son ... Somewhere his provision is happening.

Anagona of thousands of people returning to the office ...

In the meantime, someone said to me - this is the

grandfather who hears that blood is exchanged, do you know somewhere?

Telling me?
Yeah Al that sounds pretty crap to me, Looks like BT aint for me either.

Seeing the baby boy with me, I realized in my heart .. maybe the helpless woman is in some danger, so I said with a little interest ... What is the disease?

Thalassemia - or Blood Cancer?

Hearing my question, the woman did not hesitate to say that I want to get all the blood out of my son's body given by my husband!
After staring in amazement for a while,

I thought to myself .. Okay, let's have some tea!
Do you know any magic in my words, the lady agreed to have tea?

Two teas in the next shop .. I ordered a cake for the boy! Dadabhai two butterfly biscuits with three teas.

After tea, I said ... Well, sister, tell me, what's the matter?

The lady got emotional and started talking awkwardly ...

Grandpa, he must have been fifteen or sixteen years ago. We were three sisters ...
I am Mejo!

We didn't have any brothers.

My father used to work in a good private company. He used to earn good money. Who never neglected to teach us enough reading! I was not good at reading and writing ..

I dropped out of school till class eight! One day, after getting drunk, he came home and said, "You know, mother, I got your marriage fixed ...
my son works in a gold shop!" There is a house in the house.

I said I will not get married now! Hearing that, my father slandered my grandfather! I have to agree ... In front of the 20th Falgun wedding day is ripe.

The marriage started with great fanfare .. On the day of the wedding, the relatives started saying in secret that it would be better to tie the girl around the neck than to marry the boy.

I heard this but who knows why he is saying all this .. In the meantime the boy came to see me with friends to tell me the truth, I also liked!
In any case, the groom got married in cash after spending more than one lakh rupees on food and drink.

Starting from that flower bed night .. When the boy got drunk and entered the flower bed, it was almost two o'clock at night! Then day by day the boy's notoriety started to spread ...

The boy is out of work, sometimes in Delhi, sometimes in Gujarat, sometimes in Mumbai .. sometimes he comes home! How can I talk about her virtues?

After some time, I found out that my mother-in-law is not my own mother, but also my mother-in-law has an illicit relationship with my husband ...

Hear that sin but if you do not see with your own eyes, I would not believe! I can not disbelieve my own eyes.

One day in the face of a quarrel he said I stole thousands of girls like you, I would not marry you ... I just needed a few thousand so I married you because of guilt ...

The sky was falling in my head that day but I didn't cry ...

I started to find out more about the boy inside! I found out that the boy's temperament is not good and he does not survive in this shop or in any other shop for a few days ..

because whenever he gets a chance he takes some jewelery or money and comes home to the village!

After spending some time again, he found another shop! Good as a goldsmith - The manipulation of words on him is called pukka chittinbaj .. so any of his work can be done easily.

Whatever it was, I endured all sorts of irritations and pains and did housework for three or four months and then that happened ...

One morning all my gold jewelry and money went away with my husband god and did not return mother-in-law's various gossip started! I went to my father's house when I was three months pregnant.

As usual I gave birth to a boy that he is a great person ... He pointed his finger at the boys.
A few months later, my father retired ...

How does the family get a little pension money?

Boy, I was looking for a job before I was six months old, but no job survived, so here are two days, there are four days, here are six months!

Then ... by the grace of a little grandfather in the neighborhood, I got a job in a warehouse that I still do ... no less letters ...!

It's been two years since my parents died! Family expenses Rent a house - I save some money by spending on my son's education! I did not find any defect in my son's education.

When you want - eat - drink clothes - come Give everything as much as you can .. I will not be deprived if one day the boy becomes a human being like me in this hope ...!

I work hard day and night with broken bones .. I earn money by pouring blood on my body day and night, I have not taken any wrong path yet! But do you know the grief grandfather?
Everything I heard for so long was fine, then what happened?

What more can I say, Grandpa, I am saying this because you feel like your own grandfather.
He used to tell lies when he was young .. He used to tell lies and if he was in Delhi he would say Mumbai if he was in Mumbai he would say in Goa

I used to give a lot of advice about this ..
I used to beat him .. and I thought when he grows up he will understand that I am doing everything for you and he will understand my sorrow.

Absolutely not an ass? What can I say, his character is changing as he gets older! Has made new friends .. lately money is being lost from time to time ...

When I tell him, he refuses and instead he is blaming someone else .. but I know very well that no one will give me money except in my house!

This sometimes leads to unrest ... I will pay ten thousand rupees in the cupboard after getting paid on the seventh day Thousands of rupees are missing ...

A boy in class five got angry at the thought of what to do with a thousand rupees, so today is a holiday so I went out with him ...

When I was in class eight, the science sir said that people are guilty of this blood or people are good and bad ...

so I know that his father's blood is flowing in his body. In this hope ... Grandpa, do you know?
Is there any doctor who exchanges blood like this?
Do you know such a search, grandfather ???

... tears welling up in my eyes ...

What can I say with my mouth ... I think to myself that in school and college life we have read that a person's character is formed due to his genetic traits.

But if all the blood can be changed, can its character structure be changed? That is unknown to me.

Still, in a consoling voice, I said, "OK, a doctor be my friend ...
I'll ask him, please give me your phone number!" He eagerly handed me the fifty taka note with the phone number and told me to pay for the tea. When I refused to take it, he paid for the tea himself.

The lady left with a question ...

I've read a lot about archeology ...
Mendelian genetics ... Darwin's evolution, but no good answer!

If for the sake of argument it can be assumed that if all the blood of a human body is changed, does the character structure of human nature change ???

Do you know friend Be sure to let us know in the comment box ...

Finished.....

www.ingramcontent.com/pod-product-compliance
Lightning Source LLC
LaVergne TN
LVHW100336181026
850499LV00039B/1106
* 9 7 8 9 3 5 6 1 0 4 3 4 1 *